Soledad

by Eduardo Acevedo Díaz

translated by Kathryn Phillips-Miles

and Simon Deefholts

The Clapton Press

Soledad by Eduardo Acevedo Díaz
Original title: *Soledad (Tradición del Pago)*
Published by A. Barreiro y Ramos, Editor, Montevideo, 1894

Translated from the Spanish by
Kathryn Phillips-Miles & Simon Deefholts

Cover photograph by Neven Krcmarek @ Unsplash
Cover design by Gruffydd Art

First published 2025 by:
The Clapton Press Limited
38 Thistlewaite Road, London E5

ISBN: 978-1-913693-41-1

This work has been published within the
framework of the
IDA Translation Support Program

Biblioteca de Autores Uruguayos

EDUARDO ACEVEDO DIAZ

SOLEDAD

(TRADICIÓN DEL PAGO)

MONTEVIDEO

A. BARREIRO Y RAMOS, EDITOR

25 de Mayo, esquina Cámaras

1894

Contents

A Brief Note on the Author

Eduardo Acevedo was born in Montevideo, Uruguay, on 20 April 1851. He was a writer, journalist and politician.

Dibujo original de Buscasso

Journalism and Politics

Acevedo read law at the Greater University of the Republic, interrupting his studies in 1870 to join Timoteo Aparicio's revolutionary movement against the Colorado government, presided by Lorenzo Batile, which achieved a compromise peace agreement after two years of struggle.

He founded *The Uruguayan Magazine* in 1875 in opposition to the Colorado presidency of Pedro José Varela, and went into exile in Argentina after his involvement in the unsuccessful 'Tricolor' revolution. He returned after a few years but his criticism of the new president, Lorenzo Latorre, forced him back into exile.

Finally returning to Montevideo in the 1890s he founded 'El Nacional' newspaper and was appointed as Senator by the Partido Nacional. He participated in the second insurrection of Aparicio Saravia in 1897, and joined the Consejo de Estado in 1898. He undertook various diplomatic assignments in the Americas and Europe between 1904 and 1914. He died in Buenos Aires in 1921.

Literary Career

Acevedo's first novel, *Brenda*, was published in 1886, followed by perhaps his most famous literary work, *Ismael*, in 1888, the first part of a tetralogy based on the civil wars betweeen 1808 and 1825.

Soledad, his eighth novel, published in Montevideo in 1894, reflects his interest in Uruguayan rural life and the tensions between the nomadic *gaucho* lifestyle and the oppressive hierarchical discipline of the landowning ranchers.

Soledad was followed by two more novels and several collections of short stories and essays.

Select Bibliography

Novels

- *Brenda* (1886)
- *Ismael* (1888)
- *Nativa* (1890)
- *La boca del tigre* (1890)
- *La novela histórica* (1890)
- *Etnología indígena* (1891)
- *Grito de gloria* (1893)
- *Soledad* (1894)
- *Minés* (1907)
- *Lanza y sable* (1914)

Short stories

- *El combate de la tapera* (1892)
- *La cueva del tigre* (1890)
- *El molino del galgo* (1890)
- *Nidos y besos. Idilios precoces* (1896)
- *Sin lápida* (1900)
- *Aurora sin luz* (1901)

- *El primer suplicio (1901)*
- *Pasajes del paisaje (desde el tronco de un umbú) (1902)*
- *Date lilia (1902)*

Essays

- *Carta política (1898)*
- *La civilización americana. Ensayos históricos*
- *La última palabra del proscrito*
- *El libro del pequeño ciudadano (1907)*
- *Los nuestros (1910)*
- *Épocas militares en el Río de la Plata (1911)*

Soledad

by Eduardo Acevedo Díaz

Chapter One

Hidden on a mountainside, down in a ravine, a miserable little cabin was just visible. It was misshapen and delapidated, like an ovenbird's nest that the wind has covered with dry, discoloured straw. From a distance it could also be mistaken for a large burrow of *vizcachas* or foxes, being poorly situated, dark, squat and bent over like a hunchback.

The cabin was clearly showing its considerable age, with deep cracks in its adobe walls and its thatched roof the worse for wear as a result of the constant rain. It was more like a temporary shelter for a poor itinerant gaucho than a comfortable home for a humble and hard-working family.

And in fact, this building could only be clearly discerned from a birds-eye view, because although it was actually lived in, it was more like a ruin than a home, lost in the thickets and brambles of the outlying area and hanging over the deep basin of a river that snaked between banks of thorny trees.

This eagle's nest or viper's nest of prickly bushes had for some time been home to Pablo Luna, where he lived a solitary life. He was a young man with limited contact with his neighbours and no official occupation, so his lifestyle was somewhat mysterious. He was like one of those solitary mushrooms that grow on seep willows and in places overrun by thistles.

However, Pablo Luna, according to rumours, had a female companion with whom he spoke in a mixture of languages and who would sing like a blackbird in his hands, given the range and tone of sounds that he would tease from her on quiet evenings. And this companion was his guitar, 'the perfect friend for melancholy people, a friend whose very joyfulness is always a presentiment of something bad to come.'

When people spoke about him in the district, chatting at cattle branding or sheep shearing time, they said that he was a man of above average height, slim, with a girl's waist, a short, sparse, dark beard, a swarthy, slightly ruddy face, and slate-blue eyes. His hair was long and curly with a centre parting, his eyebrows were like the wings of a swallow, and his ears were as small as pink snails, while his hands were quite large and hairy. There was another particular detail: his eyelids drooped a little, lending his eyes a vague, sleepy expression. He couldn't have been more than twenty-five years old, judging from his appearance.

On public holidays he could be seen giving the local villages a wide berth, dressed
in his *chiripá* and new boots, a narrow-brimmed black hat with no chin-strap, a *poncho* worn cross-wise, a woollen vest clinging tightly to his trunk, and at his waist a wide

puma-hide belt with Spanish half-ounce gold coins serving as buttons.

He carried his guitar in his left hand, resting the soundboard against his ribs like a musket, and he had a silver-handled dagger tucked under his belt, which his right hand could easily reach with nothing more than a brisk move of his forearm; this was an object that he would handle continuously, even if only to pass the time.

He kept the fingernails on his ring finger and little finger very long and always clean, although they were tinged with amber by cigarettes, and on his ring finger he wore a plain silver ring, as thick as the hoop on a bullock's nose.

Some people noticed that the particular attention he paid to his hair did not stop a lock from constantly falling over his cheek, covering one eye, like a 'pointer to his thoughts', although many others believed this was a sign of slovenliness, his eyelid always half-closed. That curl could well have served as a humorous mark of respect for imperfection.

Pablo Luna was better known for his passion for the guitar than for the everyday activities of rural life. People had started talking about his ability to strum his guitar and sing, rather than his acts of strength and courage, but this is not to suggest that he encouraged other people to share his semi-artistic interests and pleasures. Quite the contrary, he was perhaps like a faithful mimic of a certain songbird that lives in our forests and whose most intricate songs are reserved for the times when other birds are silent and the solemn and lonely panorama is not interrupted by the flapping of wings or other inappropriate sounds.

Chapter Two

All in all, on different occasions at certain times, when passing through the valley along the side of the sierra, many people had heard the strains of a guitar played in such a way that sometimes its echoes sounded like the sonorous tones of a fine glass bell with a steel clapper, and sometimes like the low, plaintive song of a drowsy lark. At other times the strident chords made by the strings were accompanied by a hollow drumming on the guitar base, like a serenade at a witches' coven.

On other occasions, people heard soft, melancholic music, like the faint vibration of cork rubbing along the rim of a glass, that is said to resemble the sound of a solitary wasp, the 'forest crooner'.

These mysterious melodies pierced the silence of peaceful nights, when all that could be heard was the noise made by the fixed wings of insects in the depths of the valley, and the lower reaches were perfumed by the scent of myrtle and custard apples.

It was enough to hear these snatches of music at a distance, when passing across the broad plain at daybreak or at nightfall and stopping one's horse to enjoy them, for people to take away with them a pleasurable and durable experience which, later, they were unable to describe without expressing their astonishment and intense curiosity.

The 'singing gaucho', as people called him, must have spent his childhood plucking musical instruments in the thickets and learning birdsong, because sometimes he sang or whistled in such a way that it was impossible to say whether the notes and reverberations were made by a guitar or a flute, or whether it was a man whistling or a cow-bird harmonising its melodic trills with the vibrations of the guitar strings.

Aside from the music, his consummate skills were often commented upon by those who knew him or attributed them to him rightly or wrongly, with reference to two incidents, possibly the only ones in which Pablo Luna had taken part by accident, *en passant*, as he returned home after several days of roaming.

The first of these went as follows. One dark night, a group of soldiers who had not eaten for a long time were searching the plain for a hefty steer with plenty of meat that could be barbecued on a stake beside a bonfire. They went back and forth on horseback, like ghosts in the shadows, searching for a steer without success, until they came across the singing gaucho, who was casually making his way towards his cabin. Being expert in such matters, with a fine sense of smell and eyes as sharp as an owl's, he advanced along the path in the middle of the valley, woke up a steer that was sleeping in the long grass, sounded out where the rest of the cattle were lying and, giving one of them a gentle slap on its side, shouted to one of the soldiers in a loud voice: 'Cut this one's throat. You don't want to let your fire go out.' Then he disappeared immediately into the shadows. As soon as morning broke they killed the steer and it was the best meat they had ever tasted.

The second incident went like this. One afternoon, the labourers on the ranch had caught up with and surrounded a fugitive who, as his horse was exhausted, had dismounted by the forest into order to rest up in the thicket. However, by a stroke of bad luck he had caught his spurs in the brambles, ending up face down at the mercy of his pursuers. He struggled to undo his spurs, being so close to the refuge that would be his salvation. But a skilful ranch hand, eager to cut his throat from horseback with a single strike with his knife, was about to seize him by the neck, when suddenly Pablo Luna emerged from a nearby thicket, waving his guitar above his head in his right hand and shouting out at the top of his voice, 'Let him live another winter, my friend. A man is not less important than a worm!'

The ranch hand, taken by surprise, steadied his arm with his knife in the air. The fugitive's spurs broke free, taking with them two clumps of undergrowth, and he scurried off into the brambles as fast as a lizard being chased by wasps. And at the same time the singing gaucho disappeared too.

Chapter Three

Although he was withdrawn and unsociable, Pablo Luna could usually be seen at certain times of the day or night, alongside the Witch's Ravine, which was located near the ranch named after its owner, Montiel. In this semi-forested place he would dismount and continue on foot, whistling a sad tune.

Coinciding with his arrival in the district, a dramatic event had occurred which piqued Pablo's interest in a rather strange way. This sad story went as follows. One day an old woman arrived at the ranch of Manduca Pintos, located about six leagues away. She asked for employment and they engaged her to work in the kitchen. She was a poor peasant with an addled brain, who in her free time practised as a 'healer', prescribing miraculous herbs, exposing rags to the moonlight or conjuring up benign spirits. It was said that she cured rheumatics by making them 'change their step', placing one foot directly in front of the other, and people with defective eyesight by sprinkling soil on them, rather than using bandages made from lizard skin. She also practised as a vet. She restored worm-infested horses to health by tying a strip of fresh leather to their necks, and treated animals with difficulty hearing – whether bipeds or quadrupeds – by applying a snakeskin.

This sad old woman by the name of Rudecinda was always talking about her only son who, when still just a boy, had been forced to abandon his home through a combination of poverty and unjust persecution by the authorities. She had heard nothing about this son since the day he left. He was an affectionate lad with a good heart, who sang and played the guitar, and his only vice was that he was not too fond of work. Perhaps he was dead.

Rudecinda 'the Witch', as she was known, spent several months living on the Pintos ranch, but as time went on her eccentric ways began to get worse and one day she was given the sack, ruthlessly, as if she were damaged goods.

The old woman left the ranch that had been her refuge penniless, deranged and homeless. For a while, she wandered around the neighbourhood, eating roots and scraps. Later, when they set the dogs on her to force her out of her shelter in the brambles, Rudecinda left the area. A few days later she appeared on the land owned by Don Brígido Montiel, a friend of Don Manduca.

She lived in the forest, in who knows what dark burrow that she shared with wild animals. On misty evenings or moonlit nights she was often seen walking across the valley with a bundle of leftovers or scraps, or leaving the bottom of the ravine with large fistfuls of herbs and wild flowers. When the locals saw her, ragged and dishevelled, her eyes bulging from their sockets as she clutched mysterious bits and pieces close to her chest, they kept their distance, staring back at her and muttering, half scared, half joking: 'she bears the mark of the Devil'.

One afternoon, Don Manduca Pintos, who was heading towards the outbuildings at a gallop, saw her climbing out from the ravine, like a ghost. She pulled a face and tossed a large handful of strange herbs in his path. His horse took fright, and Pintos said angrily, 'Get out of here, you evil witch!' The old woman gave a hoarse cackle and went to hide in the brambles again.

A few days later, early one moonlit night, that poor woman, disarrayed, half-naked in her rags, caked in mud, her hair loose and wild and her feet bare, not so much walking as dragging herself along by the ravine, had a fight with a pack of wild dogs over a sheep's corpse. She laid into them with her fists, screaming and shouting. Then the enraged dogs, defending their carrion, started biting her, dragging her along and tearing off strips of her flesh with their fangs. They jumped on her in a pack and tore her to bits, and finally hurled her miserable body to the bottom of the ravine.

Someone who was wandering nearby heard the witch's howls, mingled with those of her assassins, and came rushing towards the sound of the fight. The man who came galloping over, riding full pelt, guided by his instincts as a nomadic gaucho, was none other than Pablo Luna. Some of the dogs were still feasting. They had eaten the sheep almost down to the bones, but the entrails still remained and all the dogs were desperate to devour them. They were standing around the corpse in a tight circle with their snouts all bloody. In their feeding frenzy they paid no attention to the horse-rider.

The singing gaucho had been observing the scene from a distance, when his horse suddenly gave a violent shudder. He looked down into the ravine and, under the bright moonlight, he could make out the emaciated body of a woman clothed in rags, half-suspended in the brambles. Pablo was not afraid and quickly dismounted. He went down and leant over the body which was lying rigid, eyes open and chest ripped out, his face almost brushing against it, and remained there for a few seconds in contemplation. All of a sudden, his whole body gave a shudder, shaking like a reed, and an intense, indescribable, desolate howl came from the depths of his throat. The wild dogs growled. Two of them came bounding over to him, apparently not sated by the terrible wounds their bites had inflicted on the old witch. Pablo's howling which was almost like the sound made by an opponent who had fallen in a fierce battle, intensified the dogs' bloodlust.

The singing gaucho, now back on his feet, unhinged and desperate, took an enormous leap and with a guttural scream and a savage thrust of his knife he stabbed one of the wild dogs clean through the heart. Now in a blind fury, the dogs flew at him in a frenzy. He teased the angry beasts with his blanket wrapped around his left arm, while with his right arm he thrust his fearsome dagger back and forth, slashing through their bodies, inflicting deadly wounds. The battle did not last long but it was furious, with no quarter given.

The remaining dogs decided to flee and they tore their way through the brambles to make their escape from the ravine, leaving three of their number lying stretched out on the ground. Pablo, ever observant, noticed that two of these were still moving, and he set about them ruthlessly, pinning their shoulders down with his gaucho boot and cutting their throats with malevolent delight. It gave him some consolation to see the blood spurt from their necks, hot and wet, soaking the ground and his hands and boots. He wiped his dagger clean on the dogs' pelts and found some clover to restore its shine. Then he gave a big sigh and rubbed his eyes on his sleeve.

His frightened horse had retreated a short distance. He went to fetch it and gave it a stroke. Then, leaning against the side of the ravine, he gathered up the witch's body in both arms. Before placing it across the saddle, he had another look at the dead woman's face and silently kissed her. Then he lifted her up, carefully placing her across the horse, and jumped up on to its haunches and headed towards the edge of the forest.

It was a splendid night. The hillside, the valley and the treetops were bathed in a pure white light. A sombre line traced the edge of the forest. The singing gaucho followed it for a long time, as if lost in his thoughts. His horse kept stopping, since it could feel no pressure on the reins until, hearing the screech of an owl resting in the branches of a tree, the rider dug his spurs into the horse's flanks and they continued their silent march.

At last, they entered a dark patch of scrubland. He dismounted and lifted down the butchered body. The soil was soft in this area owing to the humidity of the river bank. The river ran along a narrow course bordered by twisted tree trunks and a thick curtain of vegetation. A ray of moonlight pierced the darkness like a long, silver arrow and cast a spot of light over the calm water. Pablo balanced the dead body against a tree. That woman, possibly aged by constant harsh suffering over the years, worn out, emaciated, her eyes protruding from their sockets and her skin stretched across her bones, now stiff with *rigor mortis*, savaged to death by the dogs, covered in blood and coated with dust and mud, barely covered by the remains of a colourless scrap of material was, for him, an object for silent and painful contemplation.

The gaucho's distraught face bore a deep furrow of intense pain. From time to time, he grasped the dead woman's limp and wrinkled hand, studied it with a fixed stare, lifted it to his trembling lips and then suddenly let go of it as he felt its terrible coldness. Something like a solemn voice that came from the depths of his soul, like a distant echo of lost memories, seemed to tell him that they were of the same flesh, and that he had suckled at that sad, shrivelled-up breast and that her rough dry hand, with its gnarled fingers and torn nails, had guided him and kept him safe at the time when a man can only crawl and scream, unable to stand on his own feet like all the other animals in the countryside. It had to be so, that they were of the same blood, because when he looked at her, old and ragged and broken, he felt a stab in his chest, deep and penetrating, like a splinter from the cross, that only the poor witch could have dug from a wound that did not bleed but which made his guts scream with a violence he had never known before. He occasionally let out a hoarse cry, with no tears or shaking; short, spontaneous and alarming in the quiet solitude of that place, very much like the muffled snorts of a sickly bull.

He slowly looked around, carefully observing the bloody mess, detail by detail. Then he stopped and stared for a long time at the tree's dark branches, thinking. All of a sudden, he turned round, squatted down in order to take the witch's head, its hair all tangled, in both hands, and continued to study her in the minutest detail, as if morbidly fascinated by the horror of that monstruous mask. At one point he even dragged her to a patch of ground where the silver light of the night sky could shine on her.

Then it occurred to Pablo to close her eyes and mouth. He pulled her eyelids down with his fingers but they wouldn't fold since they were already cold and hard. He tried to close her mouth but her jaw fell open again. Then he bound it with a strip of cloth, like a chinstrap, tying the ends together over the top of her skull. Next, he tidied her hair, laying it over her chest, and stretched the fragments of her clothing over the length of her body, using strips of cloth to bind them together. Finally, he sat beside her and set about shredding tobacco to make a cigarette, very slowly, with his head bowed, weighed down by his cruel troubles.

Near to the river bank there was a closely knitted cluster of guava trees with large forked branches. Pablo dragged two hefty, dried out trunks down from the hill, cut off the branches and trimmed them with his dagger. Then he wrapped the body in a pair of palliasses that he took from beneath his saddle, binding them together with a strap of polished leather that was hanging from his horse's haunches, placed the dead woman on the two tree trunks and tied it on firmly with some other straps of unpolished leather. The witch weighed no more than an Egyptian mummy. Having completed his funereal task, Pablo picked up the bundle and headed towards the cluster of guava trees. He leaned the bundle against a tree trunk and took off his spurs. Then he climbed the tree, using his feet and his knees to cling to the trunk, shuffled on to a thick branch that groaned under his weight, took hold of the top end of the strange coffin and with considerable effort lifted it up and balanced it in a fork between two branches. Finally, climbing down from the tree and using his head and both hands, he pushed up the other end of the coffin until it nestled in another fork between the branches of the tree that was closest. To complete his sad task, he bound each end of the coffin tightly to the trees, so that it could not be dislodged by the wind.

Then, picking up his iron spurs, he returned slowly to the patch of trees, flung himself to the ground and began to sob. Once that moment of grief had passed, he murmured in a low voice: 'That woman was a witch, and she was truly my mother.'

He heard a light fluttering of wings among the branches. He looked up. A pair of phosphorescent eyes stared back at him, motionless, from the depths of the cluster of trees, and soon afterwards a strident screech shattered the silence. It was an *ñacurutú* owl that had landed next to the corpse, very self-assured, its large ears stiff with feathers. It was a sombre, mysterious image of the nomadic life, a gloomy companion in the hours without peace or light.

Chapter Four

The main village or hamlet attached to Don Brígido Montiel's ranch was located in the valley, about a mile away from Pablo Luna's house. Montiel was a simple man. He was short with a wide face, broad shoulders and enormous hands. His unruly sideburns joined together to form a semi-circle across his lower jaw, resembling the asymmetric bristles that cover a puma's muzzle. The fleshy parts of his ears were thick and protruding, his eyebrows bushy and unruly. A short beard and bull-like neck made up the rest of the notable features of this runaway slave, herdsman and local master of the lasso and dagger.

No one really liked him as he was so belligerent. Even when he was trying to be pleasant, a rare occurrence, people found him offensive. In this way he was like a cat. Although the men who worked for him were country people, like him, few of them had such crude instincts and rude manners. He always overdid things when it came to giving orders or criticising. People worked for him purely for the money, which he managed with a tight fist, and because of his daughter, Soledad, who was a delight; but woe betide the labourer who annoyed him or incurred his wrath: they would find neither work nor welcome there. Montiel often said that the gaucho was moulded by discipline, and by the same token it was better to snarl at him than to give him friendly advice.

Soledad was pretty and provocative, with a type of creole beauty hidden in her wildness. Don Brígido had lined her up to be the wife of a rich Brazilian whose land and cattle were just a few miles away.

She was eighteen years old, with a rosy olive complexion, large dark eyes, a curvy figure and hair so long that it fell past her waist. She was the centre of attention of all the young men in the district. Like a seductive fruit, ripened in the shade of kapok trees, or the kapok trees' own fleshy fruit, hidden away in the upper reaches, her tempting allure had captivated the passions of every man in the forest and branded its image on to their hearts, to the extent that the proudest and most rebellious of men swarmed around the place and returned to surrender themselves to Montiel's yoke, bottling up their resentment and even their vengeful instincts, in the hope of earning her favour. They all thought that she might share with them a kind word or a meaningful smile, an expression of interest or appreciation, a sideways glance at the poorest conversationist, a sigh for the best singer, applause for the handsomest rider, close attention to a favourite guitarist, or a fulsome laugh at the biggest fool. Even the common slaughterman would dream that his skill in cutting sheep's throats might predispose her in his favour.

The passions of the entire male population of the district were focussed on her. Flowers sprouted in the fields wherever she flapped her short skirt and any plant that she touched acquired miraculous qualities; if she placed a wild rose on her chest it would throw off an exotic aroma; any horse that she rode became subdued and affectionate.

The fact is that Soledad did not seem much concerned about anything around her, and even her engagement to Don Manduca Pintos, the Brazilian rancher, didn't keep her awake at night. She did what she liked and said what she liked without caring about the consequences, judging from her relaxed and scornful attitude, a sure sign of a woman with no worries or business to attend to.

She enjoyed her freedom to the full; she rode the finest horses and sometimes she danced. She paid scant attention to domestic chores and barely knew how to sew. As for moral guidance she had never learned a prayer and had no idea what a religious service might consist of, but on the other hand she was skilled at finding broody hens and ostrich nests, selecting the best ears of corn, foraging prickly pears and making stews. And not just ordinary stews. Don Brígido used to say that nobody could flavour a beef stew as well as she could, not to mention prairie oysters, a delicacy she had been fond of since she was a little girl, and which was also one of Don Manduca's favourite dishes.

Chapter Five

One afternoon, Soledad was out walking near the orchard, when she noticed someone passing by, riding a sorrel horse at a slow trot. It was Pablo Luna. She only knew him by his name and the fact that he was praised by many for his skill at singing and playing the guitar. This, together with the veil of mystery that surrounded his errant lifestyle, heightened her curiosity at the unexpected sight of him passing by just a few paces away from her. This was a rare event because he was almost never seen close to the ranch's outbuildings.

Soledad watched him go by with his head lowered, glancing at her out of the corner of his eye. He looked at her with a melancholy air, in a manner that seemed cold and disinterested. He carried his guitar on his hip, his hat tilted back, floating behind his dark curls, his face very pale but wearing a resigned expression.

As he went past he managed to stammer a 'good afternoon' and he tipped his hat. Soledad scarcely moved her head but, once he had gone by, she stared openly at his back with an expression of bewilderment and surprise. And she didn't stop staring until he eventually disappeared from sight into a large thicket near the forest. It occurred to her that he had not once returned her gaze, unlike all the ranch hands who were always making eyes at her.

What an obnoxious man! But wasn't he so handsome? There were few others like him. It then occurred to her that Don Manduca, her fiancé, was a tubby man with bandy legs and a dark-olive face, a goatee beard and his hair was already going grey. The difference between him and the singing gaucho left her a little uneasy. It was the fleeting thought of a vivacious, full-blooded young woman, whose hidden instincts might be piqued and spurred into action by any minor incident. Faced with a man so dashing and dapper, with those graceful curls, that daring youthfulness, the facial expressions of a songster, trusting in his own devices to lead an errant life, and that resigned attitude which showed in his eyes, it was impossible for her not to compare!

Even in the presence of so many other men it had not occurred to her to look at Don Manduca alongside anyone else. Now that it did occur, it was as if her feelings had been suddenly been awakened and she experienced something of a rude shock. Why was it that she had never made such a comparison, whereas now she was placing him beside Pablo Luna and noting the difference? There was little point dwelling on the reasons why. What she did know was that Don Manduca was very advanced in years and the other man was handsome and seductive.

But this Pablo Luna was so scornful and unsociable! And, holding that thought, Soledad's lip curled with a touch of irony. Then she pulled a haughty expression, made her dress flutter with a sudden twirl and, looking for one last time at the place where the singing gaucho had disappeared, she walked slowly back to the outbuildings.

From time to time she looked herself over front and back, straining her neck with a certain hint of wounded pride. In truth she was a little bit out of sorts, without realising the cause of her sudden anger. Could it be that she was learning what it was like to be in love? She had never felt affection for any man apart from her father, despite the gross manner in which he always expressed his fondness, even when it came to his daughter.

To sum up, she was pretty, glowing with youth, strong and full of youthful desires, and ready to experience a violent change in her monotonous life at the drop of a hat. Until that moment she had been like a magnet for other people's wishes, the centre of all the secret desires of those who surrounded her. And now, was it her turn to be smitten? Or at least, could she not use her charms to capture a different sort of man, with an itinerant lifestyle, like the one who had just passed in front of her eyes, indifferently, as if bored with a world that seemed to be reduced for him to the loneliness of the valley and the hills, the only consolation being the wild birds' song, the shade of the forest, the splendid light of the sun, the melancholy strumming of his guitar and perhaps the memory of a miserable adolescence? She was troubled by the singing gaucho. He wasn't the same as the others.

Why hadn't he turned to look at her before disappearing gruffly into the ravine? Was it that she was of no interest to him, that he was blind to the charms that others attributed to her? Was her face not as pretty as people said? Were her eyes not like two fireflies that lit up the paths at night? There was no doubt that his eyes were very attractive, as blue as a newly blossomed thistle flower, although one appeared to be 'droopy', making his curly eyelashes quiver.

Old Montiel, her father, said that this was 'the eye of a fraudster', an outlaw, who would swindle his way from sunrise to sunset. But that's not how he seemed to her. Don Brígido held a deep dislike for Pablo because, according to him, he survived by stealing the rancher's sheep and cattle, although nobody had ever managed to catch him in the act of slaughtering one.

This animus on the part of her father was the reason why the poor itinerant was unable to find work on the ranch, and he would give a wide berth to anyone working there on the rare occasions that he chose the nearby path. Don Brígido had verbally abused him on several occasions when their paths had crossed in the countryside or at the 'shelter', where Luna would sometimes go in search of a day's employment. The last time they met he had made some terrible threats towards him. Pablo had left, as silent as a dead man. She had heard the ranch hands talking about it and now it all came back to her.

And as she suddenly remembered it, as one remembers an event that one gave no importance to at the time, she began to think that maybe her father's animosity was unjustified, since the singing gaucho seemed to be a good sort, humble and gentle. Wasn't it true that certain big cats were like that, even though they devoured sheep? What was more, she had heard people talking about Pablo that made him seem attractive and kind, although always shrouded in mystery.

Some people claimed that, hidden between enormous peaks and gullies in the depths of the sierra, there was a cave where the singing gaucho would take a quiet siesta, while on the peaks of the mountains the eagles screeched and in the deep valleys the wild cats howled. He would pass the daylight hours in this remote cave, and when the sun had set he would go out on his horse and ride deep into the thicket. He always had his guitar strapped on his back or clasped in his right hand. He didn't play it for other people, but there in the solitude he would strum away for the delight of the mountain creatures. They added that the birds would hop down from branch to branch, crowding together on the pasture land, and that on one occasion a group of bald-headed crows sat quietly on the rocks of a gully, just a few steps away, to listen to him play. When he had finished strumming and singing, the crows flew off like a black cloud over his head, with a chorus of funereal caws.

An itinerant worker hidden in the reeds beside the

river had also witnessed some dramatic and heroic events by pure chance. One of these stories in particular eloquently revealed a strength of feeling and a show of strength that are highly unusual.

The river had burst its banks because of the heavy rains, and enormous quantities of water had streamed down from the hills, swelling the flow, and the water that burst over the banks of the ravine spread through the forest and even partially flooded the plain. The tree trunks, none of which were very high, seemed to be more than a third under water, so that the tips of the branches touched the surface. A series of green tree-tops created a decorative border to the abyss, swaying and occasionally disappearing in the valleys of the sierra. This vast reserve of uniform, homogenous local vegetation was interrupted here and there by solitary palm trees which towered over the crowd of different species, slender and graceful, like tasselled parasols.

To the inexpert eye, any sign of a ford had been completely obliterated and what looked like a dangerously deep pool had taken its place. Who would dare to cross here when the current was at full strength? Even the tallest peach trees on the river bank had disappeared under the water. So too the reeds and pampas grass, whose conical white tips only protruded an inch above the swollen river.

A *capybara*, emitting strange calls, was swimming in places which had previously been dry land and numerous flocks of ducks and swans were gathered in the gaps in the forest which had previously been fertile pastures. The huge mass of water flowed past silently, creating whirlpools in some places and in others throwing up bubbles and foam in concentric circles. Pieces of tree trunks and branches were swept along by the river, gathering pace as they approached an incline and then, like a speeding train, they plunged into a dip littered with large rocks, which served as a ford under normal conditions and which now made the water circle around at breakneck speed in five or six whirlpools. Not one of those large rocks was now visible.

A few fragments of dried leather and wool together with thorn bushes, reeds and rushes and clumps of earth stripped from the river banks combined to form a floating heap of detritus, following the course of the river like a routed army rushing headlong, seized with panic. Clusters of roots and broken branches had gathered around the trees, which were draped with long green strands of parasitical plants, deposited there by the rising waters. From a distance, this blanket of detritus looked like a hard crust, because the water there was calm. In the distance one could see the peaks of the sierra.

According to the witness, in these conditions, at midday, a horse rider, who had stopped momentarily to observe the ford, plunged into the river. This man had scarcely a thread on his back, the witness added. His horse had nothing more than a rag for a saddle and a lasso around its neck. The rider wore a neck scarf tied like a headband across his forehead, with *boleadoras* and a dagger in his belt.

Noticing that he was hesitating, the witness felt that he should warn him not to enter the ford because the current would sweep him away, but the presence of another rider who had just emerged from the plain forced him to hold his tongue. This new arrival at the ford was Pablo Luna, with his shy, sombre manner and his guitar swinging on his back.

The man with the headband splashed into the water, holding on to his horse with his right hand and using his left arm to swim at the same pace as his mount. They drifted comfortably out to the middle of the river which had now become much wider, but once in the centre of the current they were dragged a long distance away from the ford, despite the furious efforts of man and beast. Their efforts were in vain. The current was too strong to make any impression. Realising this, the man sat on the horse's haunches, trying to steer it through the current. It was a strong horse and it reared up twice, its hooves pounding the water, without breaking free from the reins.

Their descent continued and they were approaching the crossing place. They could hear the dull sound of the swirling waters. The startled horse whinnied and stretched out its neck, and its rider went pale. He turned to face the horse's rear and leaped into the river, trying to avoid the current. But he was caught by a whirlpool which made him spin like a top, and then gradually forced him sideways into the middle of the stream. He was a very strong swimmer and he still tried to fight his way across to the other bank.

Having spun around and lashed out with its forelegs, the horse was now some distance away and was no longer of any help. It broke the surface two or three times, rearing up on its hind legs, full of energy, in an attempt to drag itself through the obstacles, but it was pushed back underwater inexorably by a mysterious force. Then it sank, reappeared, gasping lugubriously for breath and spun round rapidly in the bend in the river. It had fallen and crashed into the submerged rocks. It was not seen again.

The horse's owner followed in its tracks. He had decided to float on his back, as if fighting to allow as much air as possible into his lungs, and let himself be dragged along by the current like a cork or an inflated bladder. There was no doubt that his strength was flagging. He began to sink gradually. His clenched fists would appear on the surface, desperately grasping at the mound of detritus which slipped through his fingers.

Suddenly, a man's head peered out between the almost completely inundated trees, at the edge of a very narrow rocky outcrop. The head belonged to Pablo Luna. He had clearly seen everything that had happened and, knowing the terrain, he had made his way across the branches to the outcrop, arriving at the side of the river.

Right at the end of the gap, his supple body was stretched out over a section of a branch which was gradually bending until its leaves touched the surface of the water. Firmly wedged there like a mountain cat, and with enough free space between his head and the tree, he swung his lasso above his head and hurled it towards the swimmer, who caught hold of it eagerly, wrapped it around his waist until it was taut, and held on to it with both hands. He regained his confidence and began to pull on the rope, advancing clumsily, ashen-faced, puffing like a steer that has been dragged along by a lasso for some distance with the noose around its neck.

But just as he reached the tree, the branch to which the improvised safety rope was attached broke off with a loud crack, and the man went under immediately. However, it was not long before he re-emerged a few yards downstream, his arms flailing in the air, and finally all that could be seen floating on the surface was his long hair.

Meanwhile, Pablo Luna recovered part of the lasso and secured it again with another knot. Then he leaped from the rocky outcrop and plunged into the water, stark naked. The impetus carried him straight to the side of the drowning man, who he grabbed by the hair. The man with the headband rose from the depths, as if he had just been waiting for a gentle tug, and embraced Luna. Then the two of them, clutching each other, face to face, started spinning round, sank beneath the water then reappeared, still holding on to one another, in the centre of the current.

But the current didn't carry them downstream. The lasso appeared to be tight and firm, since it was tied to the singing gaucho who gave a loud cry and seized his companion from behind, crossing his arms across his chest, grasped the rope firmly in his hands and little by little pulled himself in, despite the heavy weight he was bearing. In a few moments he had reached the trees in the gap, and disappeared into them with his burden.

Oh, dearest Pablo! As Soledad recalled this episode which she had heard straight from the mouth of the ranch hand who had witnessed it, she remembered that Montiel hated Luna out of pure spite.

Chapter Six

But then she remembered how don Manduca Pintos had treated her, as proof of his deep affection; and although she was not fully committed to the man from Río Grande, she had not considered it a big deal whether she became his wife or not. All in all, the idea was reinforced by the recollection of certain things that tied her to her *fiancé* like a yoke. She could not forget what had happened one day not far from the outbuildings, almost in the forest and close to a thicket, when she fell from her horse. On this occasion, she was given a great shock by a fully grown jaguar, which had doubtless been taking a siesta in the brambles.

This is how the adventure evolved. The jaguar looked at Soledad and could see that her fulsome flesh would make a splendid feast. It advanced a couple of steps, moving its head and tail from side to side and licking its whiskers.

Although she was partly hidden behind her horse, Soledad could sense the jaguar's proximity. She let out a stifled scream and remained frozen to the spot in shock. The uneasy horse took a few steps forward and then turned, its ears stiff and its eyes glazed, until it had moved a reasonable distance from the wild cat. Clearly, it could sense the danger. Soledad grasped the halter and pressed herself against the horse's chest, automatically following in its footsteps, too breathless to place her foot in the stirrups or call for help. Who could she call for, anyway?

Finally, the horse came to a halt, its entire body trembling, facing sideways on to the wild beast that had followed them, creeping along on its stomach as it stalked its prey. Soledad stifled a scream. Suddenly, a few paces away from them, the jaguar also stopped, twisting its tail like a domestic cat, its eyes staring with a strange glow, its haunches set like a spring.

A man was approaching along the path at the edge of the forest. He wore a *poncho* over his left shoulder and a huge dagger tucked into the back of his belt. When Soledad first saw him, he was still some distance away. All she could do was to scream hoarsely at this unexpected apparition, noticing the calm look on the man's face and the firmness of his step. Doubtless he had emerged from the nearby ravine, since she had glimpsed him earlier through the haziness of her fear. She was shaking like a leaf. She wanted to speak but the words didn't come. Instead, she smiled at the newcomer, feeling her spirits revived. Don Manduca – for he it was – shouted with a furrowed brow, 'Get out of here, you drooly spotted beast! If you don't, you'll pay dearly for it.'

And he threw back his *poncho*. It was then that Soledad watched in amazement as Pintos, with an audacity that she not thought him capable of, with one leap calmly placed himself between the horse and the wild beast, at the same time wrapping his *poncho* around his left arm and unsheathing his dagger with consummate skill.

The beast started to back off, with a stifled growl and its teeth bared, completely focussed on its opponent, blinking and occasionally running its tongue over its black lips which were dripping with drool.

Soledad did not stay to watch. Still in shock, she ran back towards the orchard, while her horse, finding itself free, suddenly took off at a wild gallop as if it had been bitten by a viper. But once she had gone a reasonable distance, hearing a faint howling, she looked back and could see the wild beast fleeing towards the interior of the forest with giant leaps over the undergrowth and generally displaying a fine physique. Don Manduca, brandishing his dagger, followed close behind with a triumphant air. All of this initially impressed her. The robust Brazilian seemed to know how to dominate jaguars, a quality she had been unaware of until he had demonstrated it before her very eyes.

That afternoon, Soledad served him his *mate* more eagerly than usual, listening to him talking with a modicum of interest, and their communal meal was very cordial. On his part, Don Brígido was extremely content to see such open expressions of happiness and hospitality.

Manduca's adventure was talked about for several days, being such an unusual event. For the ranch hands it was a talking point when it came to the siesta, and Don Manduca's stature grew more than several inches, as a sort of myth was woven around him, as one of the narrators put it. But after a fortnight Soledad had forgotten all about the episode and ended up as indifferent as before, as if she had never really felt any passion for anyone. She was more interested in discussing things relating to the countryside with the ranch hands and getting them to play the guitar than in spending time with Pintos.

When she tried to make some comment with the ranch hands or in the kitchen, everyone laughed or shrugged their shoulders. They were content to watch her sinking her fine teeth into a hard biscuit and sucking *mate* noisily through a straw, or in following all her random movements in case they might reveal some of her charms.

Sometimes she tormented them by hoicking her dress up to her knees in order to leap over the hot ashes of a bonfire, or standing in the doorway with her hands on her hips so that the sun's rays shining through her thin clothes revealed her attractive figure.

With their emotions boiling over, the ranch hands began to get jealous. They sized each other up, each of them envious of what the others had seen, which they all wanted to have admired regardless of the presence of witnesses. Jealousy made them surly and arrogant, almost envious of each other without good reason.

Being accustomed to watch quietly how the bulls in the

rodeo ring decided the question as to which of them would be the one to mate, with all the brutally suggestive strength of their bloodline and instincts, they were predisposed to emulate with their daggers what the powerful male would do with his horns. Their instincts were restrained, however, by their position in life, as well as the daily accidents on the ranch and the physical demands and exhausting nature of their work, which made them forget their petty hatreds and affections.

It was when they caught sight of Soledad that their emotions were heightened, and at leisure times, drinking *mate* and smoking tobacco, playing the guitar, singing and competing at improvising songs. It was at these times when their issues and animosity would boil over in their untamed hearts. The red mist would obscure their vision like a veil of blood. In their desire to see Soledad, they were all out early every day in the courtyard, tending to their horses.

Chapter Seven

Having seen and felt these and many other things, Soledad remembered the afternoon on which she saw Pablo Luna pass beside her. The next day she was surprised to find herself still thinking about him when she woke up, and she got up at dawn and went for a walk across the fields.

Since it was still the season for harvesting maize, a large corn-store made in the form of a conical hut had been erected near the outbuildings. It was of a medium size, with a floor covered in the cobs and dried leaves of the same plant, in order to protect the harvest from the weather. Since there was no separate space in the main building or in the extended ranch-house with its adobe walls that could serve as a store-room for the sparse crop in the period we are discussing, these corn-stores were improvised with the by-products of the plants in such an efficacious manner that the corn resisted the onslaught of the sun and also the rain and wind. Behind the corn-store there was a line of very tall prickly pear cacti loaded with fruit.

This is where Soledad headed. She went from one side to the other, spending a lot of time weighing up the fruit. Then she went into the corn-store and began to tear down the hanging leaves without any thought for what she was doing.

During one of his stays at the ranch, Don Manduca had built the store with his own hands, so as not to appear to be lazy. She was well aware of that. By tearing at the stalks and cobs she managed to make a hole in the ceiling, and when she noticed the damage she began to laugh heartily, and she left the store in good spirits.

Behind the line of prickly pears there was a large hill. She strolled towards it hesitantly, walking back on herself and weaving left and right. The day was beginning to break. It was already hot and sultry.

Close to the Witch's Ravine, almost in front of the forest, there was an isolated stretch of high pasture land, brimming with fruit trees and herbs, including wild peach, fennel and hemlock. There was also celery growing among the rocks, blackberries in the scrubland, guava on the hillside and anchor plants where there was sandy soil.

Soledad paused before entering the scrubland, lost in her thoughts. A hundred shiny insects buzzed around her and in the boughs of the trees and fronds there was a noisy swarm of beetles, bugs, caterpillars and locusts. All of these things caught her attention but, glancing towards the outbuildings to check whether she could be seen or not, she then quickly took a narrow path across the ravine and, moving at the same pace, she climbed rapidly to the top of the hill.

From this vantage point she could look over a vast terrain. The sierra was close by with its deep blue sky, its dark foothills and its yellowish peaks forming an immense curtain, edged by the green line of the forest.

Over the shimmering mountain peaks the clouds, like spirals of soft cotton, evaporated under the heat of the sun, and a splendid morning radiated its glow over the lower slopes – already clear of mist – leaving everywhere tinted with golden reflections.

Soledad began to look towards the foothills of the sierra, genuinely wild places, where a poor gaucho's dark cabin could just be seen in the midst of the thickets. But she could not make it out, because she then turned her gaze to the end of the valley to her left, between the forest and the hillside. A herd of mares was frolicking there in pastures, their tails full of burrs, gruff and steamy, almost aggressive. A stallion, impetuous and feisty, with thick bristles and a scrawny coat, was showing his teeth and shaking his mane, kicking out in all directions. The young mares milled around the matron, whose bell rang out from the centre like a military call to arms.

Finally, the impetuous stallion stopped, bowed his neck with extreme elegance, rose up with a vigorous impulse and seized a pair of rounded buttocks between his forelegs with intense and brutal care, whinnying bravely, his mane standing on end, his fetlock quivering, his nostrils wide open as if about to emit a burst of fire.

Soledad observed the scene closely, showing no sign of surprise but with a certain interest, her gaze fixed and her cheeks burning. Her breast occasionally heaved quite violently.

She walked on a few paces with her eyes on the ground and then looked up again at the foothills of the sierra, staring for a long time towards Pablo Luna's cabin, as if she were expecting to glimpse something that might relieve her sense of anxiety. Finally, she could make out a shape in the distance, that of a horse rider who had just left his home and was heading into the sierra at a canter. It could only be the singing gaucho, since he did not have any friends and nor did anyone visit his abode. But what could he be doing up there in the hills?

Maybe he would bring his guitar – his only friend – and try to captivate the hearts of other young women with his strumming, always accompanied by pretty lyrics? Soledad was mortified by this thought. It was essential that he should visit her and do the same thing, pursue her and make her fall in love.

In recent days she had felt as if she were surrounded by a vacuum and that solitude was not just her name but something that she carried inside her. She was suddenly struck by a touch of angst, something she had never felt, stirring jealousy in the depths of her heart which was full of raw instincts. A poisonous worm seemed to bite her there in her guts with a cruel persistence.

The stallion was still running with the herd and letting out its highly-charged neighing, prancing and gnashing of teeth. This began to irritate Soledad, who went back towards the prickly pears with long strides. 'I'll have to tame him!' she said to herself, her vision clouded by a strange lament that she could not suppress and which she felt in her eyelids. 'Why not? He's no different from the rest.'

Chapter Eight

That afternoon she saw him again. Luna was walking along the valley and he greeted her curtly. Her whole body quivered and she went very pale, choking with emotion which she was unable to resist. But she did not feel strong enough to look him in the eye, which deep down was what she wanted to do. On the contrary, she turned her back on him and started to walk among the prickly pears, on the pretext of choosing some ripe fruit.

She began to fumble with the fruit, charged with emotion. Her black fringe fell over her bright eyes, her eyes felt damp, her lower lip began to swell like a ripe chilli pepper and her cheeks looked like a bunch of red roses. Her whole being felt extremely uneasy. She presented all the symtoms of a panic attack, something that came with her temperament. On more than one occasion the ranch hands, observing her with covetous eyes, had exclaimed, 'You're twitching like a blue-arsed fly!'

Moving from one prickly pear to the next, deft hands avoiding the poisonous thorns, her arm moved up and down like a wild bee moves up and down in a jar of syrup. Occasionally she paused in front of a tempting piece of fruit. But she had a hard, inflexible head, and all she did was shake her mane of hair, without turning round.

Finally she lowered her trembling hand almost to the

hem of her dress, which had caught on one of the dark-green thorns; she took hold of it and yanked it halfway up, exposing a leg that was so finely formed that, when she went to cover it up again she gave a satisfied smile, displaying a hint of pride on her lips, aided by the conviction that she had struck a blow to his heart.

Seeing this, Pablo Luna brought his horse closer, and remained there staring at her, eyes wide open. Then he advanced a few paces, not in a straight line, but zig-zagging like an ostrich, dragging his horse whip over the vegetation or using it to flick a locust that was taking off in front of him, exposing its burnished wings to the sun.

He managed to get very close to her and she also played her part, perhaps without realising it, each of them attracted to the other by an impulsive force. And once they were close neither of them said a word, and they took a few steps back, turning round without looking at each other except in sideways glances, as if there were no empathy between them and they had been struck dumb by some awful accident.

They went back and forth. He pushed his hat back in order to wipe the sweat from his brow. She threw a barbary fig on the ground as if angry with its thorns and turned back to the prickly pear bushes. Pablo followed her in spite of himself. Seeing her brimming with youth and moving around feverishly, he felt the blood coursing through his veins and an unfamiliar desire to talk or sing or smile, so that she would listen to him or look at him without contempt or indifference. This unsettled him and made him hesitate.

Then Soledad came up close to him, so close that he thought he could feel the warmth from her face. She puckered her lips in a sensual expression and finally said to him in a very low voice: 'The figs are too warm . . . when you bite into them they melt into juice.'

Soledad pulled a face and shook her thick plaits, and laughed without looking at him. Then she brushed past him and bent down to do up a shoelace that had become loose. She placed a small blue flower in her mouth, gripping the stalk between her teeth. Pablo Luna watched her from one side, without moving, and murmured as if he were talking to himself, 'Who wouldn't want to be a flower!'

At that very moment he heard the ranch owner's voice, shouting from a window, 'There's that bloody tramp again. Go back to your slum, you dirty vagrant!'

Hearing this, Pablo saddled his horse without saying a word, mounted up and headed back to his cabin, his chin buried in his chest and his feet not touching his spurs. Soledad watched him with a sad look on her face.

Chapter Nine

A few days later the shearing season started and there was hard work to be done on the ranch. Piece-workers had come from far and wide until a quota of thirty workers was filled. Almost all of them were men highly skilled for the job, who would not take on any other type of work and who would wander from pillar to post, or from ranch to ranch as they would say in the countryside, until the hot weather arrived and the fleece was smooth and ready to be shorn.

Picture the scene: frenetic activity, extreme heat and a sultry atmosphere beneath a large canopy. Bodies stooped over, arms moving ceaselessly, sheep laid on their sides, numerous lambs, the sound of metal on metal and hoarse, breathless voices, pitiful bleating after multiple pinches from the shears, tangles and bristles standing on end, the occasional burst of hearty laughter, buckets of sweat, sheep dragged brutally along the ground by their legs, extraordinary gymnastics by the sheep that had already made their contribution, prancing about, white sheets with the occasional red lesion wrapping round them like a belt, wiggling their tails and protesting loudly, the whole flock filling the air with monotonous echoes reverberating around the fine, cinnamon-coloured dust, hasty round-ups and complaints from the obnoxious foreman buzzing around like a bumble bee from corner to corner and back to the centre, always menacing with his tongue as sharp as a lancet, mastiffs sleeping the siesta by the edge of the undergrowth, snoring away without a care in the world.

The air smelled of nothing but sheep. The sound of the shears and the lambs' bleating combined to make music that was rhythmless and strident. Like the discharge from a malign fever, everyone breathed mouthfuls of stale breath from numerous men and beasts. Under the blazing sun, shimmering in the distance over the still upper pastures, several thrushes, their beaks half-open, flew through the air in search of some fronds in which to shelter, their humid wings at full stretch.

Among the shearers was Pablo Luna, eager and focussed. He had arrived very early and asked the foreman for a pair of shears, telling him, 'Even if it's for a pittance, I want to work. Don't reject me.'

'OK,' the foreman had replied, 'but keep an eye out for the boss. If he finds you here he'll kick you out without any discussion. He's in a bad mood today and he nearly gave me a dressing down already.'

As mentioned earlier, Don Brígido Montiel was very short and somewhat tubby. Perhaps because of this and his bitter, aggressive temper, the foreman considered him no better than a skunk.

As soon as the singing gaucho entered the open shelter he set to work, without a word to anyone and not lifting his head except on the rare occasions when his work made it necessary. He didn't ask for his pay. The other ranch hands observed him without saying a word, perplexed, and exchanged a few words with each other under their breath. Pablo Luna, in spite of this, carried on as if totally absorbed in his work, his hat pulled down over his eyebrows, and with a fervour that astonished the foreman. He sheared twice as many sheep as anyone else.

The hours passed and toward the end of the day Don Brígido arrived at the shelter after doing the rounds. As he got off his horse, with his vulture-like gaze he took in the scene in all its detail, and tethering his horse he shouted out gruffly: 'There's one too many workers here. That one who's hiding under his hat, keeping his head down for the sake of it – I don't need him, Don Sandalio. Tell him he's fired, right now!'

The foreman tried to blurt out some excuse or other, scratching his head with one hand and placing a half-smoked cigarette behind his ear with the other. But the boss did not let him speak, raising his voice in a bitter tone, incoherent and loaded with vicious insults.

'Get him out of here. I don't want a list of excuses, you old fool! I'm sick of these wild dogs and their wily schemes. I'll set the mastiffs on these ruinous foxes, given half a chance. Let them hunt squirrels and glow-worms, the lazy sons of bitches.'

Don Brígido Montiel seemed be overwhelmed by fierce anger. Meanwhile, the ranch hands, somewhat astonished, carried on with their work in silence, with sideways glances at the boss and Pablo Luna, who had got to his feet sombrely, adjusting his belt and his *chiripá*, and making his exit slowly and without a murmur. But this time, as he moved off, he gave a hard stare at the man who wounded him so often. He brusquely tilted his broad-rimmed hat to one side and sighed loudly, perhaps from fatigue, or maybe from bitterness.

The ranch hands exchanged looks with one another. One of them said in a low voice: 'That man has been seriously insulted.'

Someone else added in the same tone, 'There's no such thing as a gentle parrot when someone yanks his tail.'

Chapter Ten

Pablo spent the rest of the afternoon and evening lying down in his cabin, until nightfall. He couldn't sleep so he got up from his bed, which was made from saddle blankets, saddled his horse and, jumping up, followed the path along the edge of the forest, heading towards the Witch's Ravine. It was only a short distance from here to Montiel's ranch. He didn't know why he was heading in this particular direction. Somewhere deep in his soul was a vague image of Soledad.

It was a calm night, the lukewarm air saturated with woodland aromas, replete with subtle shafts of light and fireflies flitting through the leafy tree-tops. The river banks were lined with trees, and the river itself spanned the whole length of the valley, leading down to the sparse land near the watering holes, then disappearing between two hills, like a huge military column on a silent march.

At that point of the river bed the water splashed down over the rocks, producing a dull noise similar to the thud of an out-of-tune drum. The only sounds in the forest were the occasional warbling of a lark, an owl hooting or the gentle song of a thrush, half-asleep in the branches of a tree, emerging from the silence like mysterious flourishes. Above the clusters of thick leaves a multitude of lightning bugs and fireflies formed a flurry of sparks amid the tree-tops, like bright green sequins reflecting the fragile light from the stars.

Pablo Luna passed the ravine and climbed up to the top of the hill. All the local settlements could be seen from this point, down to the smallest detail. They were very close. Dinner time had come and gone a while back, and there were several people taking the night air beyond the prickly pears, bare-headed and in shirt sleeves.

A woman had walked past the row of cacti and was strolling slowly towards the hillside. Pablo, who was close by, in a dark recess where the sporadic light from the houses' lanterns didn't reach, recognised this woman as Soledad. Then he went down to the stretch of land alongside the Witch's Ravine. This area was also in shadows, however, there was enough starlight to enable his countryman's eyes to see everything. Luna dismounted and tied up his horse. Soledad reached the top of the hill. She looked around, saw him and remained silent.

Pablo started to whistle softly in such a refined and pleasant way that several little birds on the hill also started chirping, unsure whether dawn was already upon them. Soledad wandered for a short while along the top of the hill, looking towards the settlements. Then she paused again, turning her back on the valley.

The singing gaucho continued his wild bird whistles, becoming more and more melodic and harmonious, with a hint of guitar strings and heart-felt laments. Then he stopped whistling, so that she could hear him speak.

'A small favour for a man who is leaving this region. May everyone enjoy a hundred years of good luck. I'll never return!'

Soledad came down the hill. She appeared to be upset by that complaint and that farewell. Once she was close up to Pablo she exclaimed, full of pride, 'So that's why you came here? Even if you want to, you mustn't leave now.' Then, in a different tone of voice, she added, 'What is it you're after? You've never even looked at me.'

'That's just it. If I didn't look at you before it was because I was afraid of being a pest. But now I can't help it. I either have to look at you or go somewhere else.'

'You don't need to go away. You are your own man.'

'OK, then I'll stay until I'm told to leave.'

'Good. But don't you realise that it's up to you what you do?'

Pablo Luna opened his eyes wide.

Soledad sat down on the grass, grabbed a handful and threw it at the singing gaucho, looking annoyed. And with that extraordinary gesture she suddenly felt a wave of happiness going straight to her head like a cloud of hot mist. Soledad stretched out on the ground, turned around and burst out laughing, throwing another fistful of grass in his face.

'You're like an untamed mare!' said Pablo stifling a flirtatious chuckle, his whole body shaking.

'Sit down here,' she said, patting the ground with her hand.

The singing gaucho flopped to the ground next to Soledad and stayed there in the same position, still laughing nervously, his hat slung around his neck and his lock of hair falling over his eyes, quivering. The two of them sat there looking at each other for a long while. In the distance they could hear Montiel's gruff voice talking to the foreman about the tasks of the following day. There was no other noise to disturb the silence, apart from an occasional whinny from the foals in the valley.

Soledad, who had been listening carefully, suddenly raised her hand and brushed the lock of hair from Pablo's face, murmuring, 'You'll end up with a squint!'

Ignoring her remark, as if absorbed in himself, he replied, 'Today I saw some crows feasting on the corpse of a wormy old nag . . .'

'And what does that mean?'

'The witch who was killed here by the dogs was insistent that it's a bad omen, even if you tie a leather cord around its neck.'

When he mentioned the witch, there was a strange tone in Pablo's voice. Soledad sat up all of a sudden and grasping Pablo by the neck with both hands she pulled him down beside her, in the same way that puppies romp and play.

'My goodness,' said Luna, with a welcome like that, we

can forget about the blessed virgin!'

And, becoming more excited, he added, 'Let's ride away on my horse.'

'No,' replied Soledad, trembling. 'There's plenty of time to run away.'

'It seems to me that the keeper of the harem has given you the evil eye!'

'Why do you say that?' she asked, laughing again, half amused and half shocked. 'All I have to do is serve him his mate . . .'

Pablo suddenly became more excited. He stretched out his arm, grabbed her by the shoulder and threw her forcefully on to the grass. Soledad did not put up any resistance, remaining there face up, calm, gentle and inviting, despite the rough handling. One of her plaits had fallen across her pretty face like a black ribbon. Luna moved it to one side with his lips and kissed her on the mouth five or six times. Then he clasped his arms around her waist, breathing heavily, and drew her towards himself impetuously, squeezing her tightly for a long while until she complained. Then he let her go.

But since she did not stand up and instead stroked his chin with the palm of her hand, Pablo clasped her again in earnest, and grasped one of her round, fleshy shoulders between his teeth.

'You're hurting me, you brute,' said Soledad in a low voice. He stopped biting her, and burst out laughing, like a child.

She got to her feet, rearranged her plaits and went off without saying goodbye. But she was slow to leave, as if reluctant to do so, hesitating and sighing. She stopped on the hillside. Just at that moment, from higher up the hill, she heard Don Brígido's hoarse voice, saying, 'There's you out for a walk, while Don Manduca is waiting to see you. He's just arrived, and the first thing he did was ask after his *fiancée*. Hurry up, you bad girl.'

'Don't have a go at me,' Soledad snapped back, showing her distaste. 'Let him wait!'

'Oh, so let him wait! Well, that's a snub and a half!'

'It's not a snub, and why should I care anyway?'

'You're getting too big for your boots, Solita. Gallivanting around with that forest peacock.'

And, with these words, Montiel went down the hill to where his daughter was standing, while she tried to place herself so that he could not see the singing gaucho. In spite of her efforts to hide him and to drag Don Brígido away, her father noticed Pablo and gave him a hefty slap, following up with two swift punches, without saying a word, as if his pent-up fury had left him speechless.

Luna, who had been almost squatting down, listening to their voices without making a sound, did not have time to stand up, and was dealt an unexpected punch in the head which left him dazed.

'Scum of the earth!' Don Brígido roared at him, almost

choking with rage. 'Count yourself lucky that I'm not carrying a knife, you bastard, because I'd happily spill your guts.'

But when he went to punch him again, a nervous hand gripped his arm, and his daughter's voice rang loud and sharp in his ear, 'Don't hit him, *papá*.'

Chapter Eleven

After Montiel struck him, Luna felt the blood rushing to his head in a flood, and once he recovered from the shock he was tempted to reach for his dagger. However, the temptation passed when he saw Montiel walking away. His daughter had grabbed hold of his arm and dragged him towards the cluster of outbuildings, along with a flurry of comments, threats and crude reproaches.

Pablo threw his arms around his horse's neck, sobbing unconsolably. He could barely stand up. His gentle horse moved forward, champing at the bit and then turned to one side, moving in semicircles, as if inviting his master to mount. Pablo appeared to be hugging him in his anguish, as if he were his only friend. Finally, he mounted and went off along the edge of the forest. He stopped suddenly by the Witch's Ravine, and stretched out both his hands towards it, in a gesture that was both strange and lugubrious.

Without uttering a word, he continued on his way, meandering through the shadows, alone with his instincts in the rough scrubland, without a clear thought in his head, his fleeting moment of pleasure embittered by the severity of the insult he had received and wrapped up in his pain. It was the same path that he had followed previously, when he had carried the witch's corpse on his shoulders; the same witch that he appeared to have reason to love beyond the grave.

He continued for a long way until he arrived at the dense patch of thicket. He quickly dismounted, adjusted his saddle with a trembling hand and burst into tears. Then he raised a clenched fist, conjured up the witch's phantom in a loud voice and, hurling himself to the ground face down, he stayed there in the same position, as if he were trying to hide his face beneath the ground. In between his lugubrious moans he uttered the word *mamá*, with a sort of reverence that was almost religious. The corpse, wedged between rough logs, seemed to be the focus of his emotions, since it frequently attracted his gaze.

His mind wandered back to the bad omen – the black crows that he had seen on the rump of a diseased animal – and the *ñacurutú* owl that served as a guardian of the suspended coffin. In this state of mind, his arms and legs shaking, he pressed his face into the soil, shaking his spurs.

He finally managed to sleep, but after a couple of hours he woke with a start, wild-eyed and his hair unkempt. He looked all around with a certain sense of unease. He took a few unsteady steps with his hands outstretched. Doubtless still dreaming, in his muddled head he saw a blood-drenched ghost with deep wounds showing through her torn rags, a ghost being chased by a pack of starving dogs, swift monsters with hackles raised and sharp teeth.

Running a hand across his eyes he drew his dagger halfway out of its sheath, examined it meticulously, like a somnambulist, and finally came back to his senses. He sat there, lost for words. The witch's body was laid to rest among the trees; next to it, motionless, the owl stared at the dejected gaucho, its eyes like two large saucers.

He flung himself back to the ground and remained there without moving for a long period. His horse wandered back and forth, restrained by the halter wrapped around its master's arm, and occasionally it bowed down and shook its head, panting. Eventually all this huffing and puffing made him lift his own sore head, and he turned to look at the hanging coffin and the owl that was staring at him in silence. In his distress he imagined that the owl's round eyes were no longer reflecting a yellow light, but rather a red glow that pierced his eyes like a flaming dart.

He got to his feet, babbling incoherently in an incomprehensible language, as if he were conversing with the witch's ghost. In between all the words that flowed from him instinctively, he carried on calling her 'mother'. Finally, he pointed his outstretched arm towards the patch where Rudecinda was sleeping her eternal rest, and waved goodbye. The owl, in turn, flapped its wings noiselessly, as if they were made of felt. Pablo also waved goodbye to this feathered guardian which protected the poor dead woman from insects.

He jumped back on his horse and set off again. But he did not head towards his cabin. He meandered through the valley, along the river beds and the watering holes, examining the paths and the ford across the river, then returning along the same route, dismounting here and there and rushing around mysteriously like a woodland elf. The hours flashed past as if they were only seconds and daybreak found him in a hideaway in the forest, with a grim expression and fierce look on his face. His head hurt and there was a dull buzzing in his ears.

'I'm turning into a wasp,' he said to himself, half delirious and pummelling his temples. Once the sun had risen high in the sky he fell asleep. He didn't sleep much, stretched out on the grass, but he stayed there until siesta time, when the sun's rays beat down from directly overhead, the atmosphere becomes oppressive, the fields of straw in the depths of the valleys look like small lagoons, the crested screamer spreads its wings over the steaming marsh, and an invisible world of insects create a form of music, the bothersome cicada reigning supreme from amongst the bushes like a chorus of flutes.

That was the time that Pablo chose to move. He was certain not to be seen, because at this time of laziness and drowsiness everyone would be asleep under the shade of the trees or beneath the shearing canopy.

He made his way through the forest, step by step. He went down into the valley, full of herds of cattle. After a certain distance he stopped and studied the surrounding terrain, seemingly vague and unfocussed. For several moments his gaze settled on certain spots with very dense thickets.

The soil was very rich and fertile in that valley. There had been abundant rain at regular intervals during the previous season and the water had penetrated deep into the soil, which had a dark, fertile layer on top, in places gently undulating as a result of overspills from the river. Elsewhere there were also small stretches of marshes covered in reeds, waxy nightshade and other very dry wetland plants.

The grass, clover and foxtail had grown immeasurably, rising up in huge clusters above the other plants. There were millions of yellow-green wild flowers of all different kinds, topped off with spikes, plumes and spherical blooms, thistles with blue flowers, clumps of withered hemlock and the dark branches of willow trees. In the centre of the valley the vegetation was tall enough to hide the cattle's bellies.

The area set aside for sheep was on the opposite side of the valley to the village. A few ostriches wandered through the dense undergrowth we mentioned, but only their heads and a part of their long necks were visible.

Pablo Luna scrutinised the landscape as if it were the first time he had noticed it. Then he rode back to his cabin. His face bore a sinister expression. He seemed absorbed by a persistent idea, or gripped by the force of terrible instincts. It was easy to guess what was happening inside his head from his fierce stare and the bitter expression which made his mouth twist. His exasperation made him grind his teeth even when he was asleep, but at the moment we're referring to he was grinding them much more than usual.

He paused in front of his shabby cabin and looked out again across the valley, at the ranch-house in the distance with its yard and corrals, the sea of wild flowers, the maize field beyond, at everything that stood out under the rays of a splendid sun. And after looking for a long time, he shook his head from side to side and let out a hoarse cry.

He jumped down from his horse, unsaddled it and sat down in the shade on a cow's skull. Then he started shredding tobacco with his knife, spending a long time on this task, pausing occasionally to rest his arm on his knee and stare at the ground in a deep depression. His shiny black curl fell over his sweaty cheek, cloaking his droopy eyelid, and from time to time he flicked it back with a jerk of his head. Finally, studying the valley once more with a grim expression he cried out, 'Skeletons, worms and dry pasture!'

Chapter Twelve

Suddenly, feeling hungry, he jumped to his feet and gathered together a pile of thick dry tree trunks, making a huge bonfire in front of his cabin, something he rarely did. He spent a considerable time on this task, since first he had to set light to a fistful of kindling with his tinderbox. Then, from inside the cabin, he brought out a hunk of mutton from a sheep he had gutted the previous day, near the hillside, and threw it on to the burning timbers, turning it over several times until the fat was dripping over the ashes. Deciding that it was ready when it was semi-rare, he started eating it, cutting off mouth-sized chunks with his dagger, drawing it in a straight line across his mouth.

Having satisfied his stomach, he set about a new task. He took a few pieces of fat from an old, perforated linen bag that was lying in a corner of his cabin, and cut it into smaller, thinner pieces with his dagger. Then he tore the bag up into strips and tied all these bits and pieces into four small bundles which would catch fire from the smallest spark from a flint. Simmering with anger, he wrapped them up carefully in a handkerchief.

He left the cabin, took a deep breath and surveyed the valley, and before long fell back into profound contemplation. Something was seriously worrying him. Then he spluttered out Soledad's name.

Half an hour later, during which time he had alternated between sitting with his face buried in both hands and pacing anxiously up and down, occasionally leaning his head against the walls of the cabin, he seemed to have found a certain sense of calm, like someone who has come up with a practical plan and found the necessary means to implement it in full, however difficult it may be. That is what must have happened in the deepest recesses of his brain, which had earlier been so agitated because, taking up his guitar, he began to strum it in a masterly fashion and then started to sing, in a sweet voice reminiscent of a poorly song-lark. The solo concert did not last for long. All of a sudden he placed the guitar next to the handkerchief bundle and stretched out face down under the eaves of the cabin. It didn't take long for him to fall asleep.

He woke up late, after the sun had dropped below the horizon formed by the peaks of the sierra, and only a hesitant glow allowed the features in the valley to be made out. An almost lukewarm, northeast wind was blowing with intermittent gusts that, while not too strong, made the tree-tops bend over and the reeds on the river bank sway from side to side.

Pablo Luna calmly saddled up his horse, meticulously placing each layer on its rump. He secured the saddle strap well and placed the lasso carefully on its hind quarters, tied his thick woollen *poncho* to the saddle straps together with a chunk of mutton and a flask.

He wound his *boleadoras* around his waist, beneath his sash, and placed the handkerchief on top, with its four bundles bound together in a row, as in an ammunition belt, his dagger to one side with the handle protruding and his guitar strapped across his back. He gently patted his horse.

After doing all this he rested. The night was closing in. A few clouds in the shape of mountains projected their shadows across the valley, creating large black outlines against the same dark background, so that it would have been difficult for the keenest eye to distinguish any object.

After ten o'clock, the singing gaucho climbed on his horse and went down into the valley, heading for the edge of the forest. This was the hour when foxes screamed and crows cawed. Apart from these sounds, perfect calm reigned.

Pablo did not hurry his mount, holding it to a steady trot for a long while, without stumbling, trusting in the silence and mystery of the countryside. He slipped under the curtain of the forest like a woodland elf. Finally, he came to a halt at the Witch's Ravine, where it was wider and the undergrowth was more tightly packed. Not a sound disturbed the quietness of this deserted place.

The singing gaucho dismounted and took out one of the fuses that he had tied up in his neck scarf. He went down into the ravine, forced his way into the undergrowth and lit the fuse, sparks spreading to the hemp which was wrapped around the core. He blew on it for a few moments until the flame took, then he placed it deep in the undergrowth and returned to where he had left his horse.

A few minutes later, the undergrowth was throwing out thick smoke, and then red flames began to appear in the gaps in the thicket. Pablo Luna mounted his horse and hastened his way to the valley, at full gallop. It was almost a race, the noise of the horse's hooves muffled by the thick vegetation.

A mile away from the ravine, the expert rider brought his horse to a sudden halt, at a place where an outlaw could have hidden in broad daylight owing to the height and robustness of the vegetation. Pablo did the same thing here as he had done in the ravine. Another fuse was set alight and simultaneously the surrounding pastures caught fire at a startling pace. Then he was off again, this time even faster, racing towards the centre of the vast plain. Here the fire had more than enough fuel. As well as the extensive pastures there were patches of wild grass and numerous bushes, most of them tinder dry. Luna set light to this in the knowledge that it would all soon be black ashes, then headed to the outskirts of the sierra, at the foot of which was the area planted with maize.

With his night vision as sharp as an owl's he found the place he was searching for, despite the fact that it was still pitch-black, scaring off the cattle that were snuffling around the edges, and a short while later a vibrant light could be seen rising from the wild grasses.

When he took up the reins again, spurring on his horse which was bathed in foam, the countryside was flooded with an intense brightness and the animals, gathered together in large groups, began to move restlessly from one place to another, with gentle mooing and whinnying, a prelude to the enormous roar that would shortly follow as the fire took hold.

The singing gaucho dug in his spurs on both sides, riding full pelt to the opposite side of the forest, where his cabin was to be found.

Between the forest and the valley there was a bare patch that served as a path, which Luna always chose for his excursions and this was the only one, apart from the path through the ravine, that could allow the inhabitants of the ranch to escape from the flames. Pablo's cabin was not far from this path. All he had to do was to pass by the watering holes and a few patches of thicket in order to be right in the centre of it, dominating the exit. This appeared to be his aim because he pressed on without stopping in order to gain time.

His horse soon reached the lower slopes of the foothills, eating up the distance and flying along the path that skirted the forest, and stopped his frenetic gallop of his own volition almost at his own doorstep. The spectacle that one could see in its entirety from this height was impressive. Pablo himself felt a huge shudder in all his extremities, which he managed to overcome with a fit of rage.

Chapter Thirteen

The high pastures and fields of long grass were burning across a wide terrain, throwing out a vivid light across the high reaches of the hillsides. Enormous tongues of snaking flames rose over the area contained by parallel rows of rocky hills. The species that flourished most there was the giant sedge which formed dazzling corollas accompanied by a faint sputter and millions of sparks.

The cattle trampled over terrifying stretches of smouldering embers as they fled. They seemed to be seized by a form of vertigo. Their hooves raked up and shredded the embers, kicking them backwards, making whirlwinds of burning ashes. Many of the bulls, their manes and tassels charred, bellowed gruffly as they made their way forward, crammed together on doom-laden paths, their horns clashing and adding to the clamour of trees exploding under the pressure of boiling hot sap.

As the terrified herd continued their formidable charge, smaller beasts that had not had time to shelter on the banks of the river ran alongside, hemmed in by the flames, and the smell of charred wool mingled with that of burnt pigskin and hundreds of wild plants consumed by the voracious fire, enormous plumes of black smoke accumulating in the sky, sprinkled with disparate sparks.

The lower slopes of the sierra, at other times cast in

shadows, now seemed to be coated in velvet the colour of blood, embroidered with the lustre of ashes, propelled by gases to float in dense clouds over the gullies and watering holes. The lower and upper peaks, wounded by the vivid reflection of the fire, stood out from the ground like hideous warts, with red and yellow tints.

In the midst of that unbreathable atmosphere, full of vapours and noises and shooting stars, the baying and whinnying, however deafening, did not drown out the men's animated cries, which rose like sharp notes in their heroic struggle with the fire.

The field of ripe maize, as if in the centre of a battle front, made a deafening noise, crackling away as the cobs opened up to reveal rows of kernels. In the elbow of a valley a herd of wild mares lined up in the form of a horse-shoe, with their haunches facing the place where the fire was fiercest, raining kicks at the flames which were approaching at a terrifying speed. These animals, their manes tangled, terror in their eyes and nostrils flared like the rings on a gas stove, their hides covered in foams of sweat, had come to rest beside some steep rocks with deep cracks, from which a multitude of thorny bushes with short, sturdy branches protruded like harpoons.

Easily combustible, this tangle of bushes had already been reached by some burning sparks, launched from some distance with the force of munitions. The thicket began to crackle and several licks of fire spread out from the doom-laden bushes, followed by a plume of smoke. Ferrets and lizards scattered everywhere, looking for somewhere to bury their heads, finding and abandoning their caves with an astonishing speed. Colonies of bats flew speedily through the smoke, screeching as they went. In the dark entrances of certain caves, crowds of other bats flapped their wings, colliding with each other in their haste to escape, collapsing in heaps a few paces from the embers.

Pablo Luna watched as a group of herdsmen arrived out of nowhere at the place where the mares were located, not far from his cabin, bravely facing the danger, throwing a lasso at one of the mares and taking her down to the ground.

They killed her on the spot, used their knives to open her up from her chest to her stomach so that half her entrails fell out, tied a lasso to one of her forelegs and another to one of her hindlegs and spurring on their horses began to drag the heap of meat and bones over the burning fields.

They took separate routes across areas that the fire had not yet dominated, dragging their bloody spoils like a curved harrow over the fire and putting it out in several stretches, displacing it to either side without diminishing its violence.

In the wake of this gloomy train there remained a few dark spots surrounded by flames. The singing gaucho, unmoved as he watched these desperate efforts, murmured: 'It's going like a rocket. You can tie down a wild mare but you can't tie down the wind!'

In fact, a strong north-west wind was blowing, pushing the flames towards the shearing canopy and the orchard, which were a short distance from the outbuildings.

Pablo Luna had chosen a good opportunity to maximise his plan of destruction. A complete disaster seemed inevitable in a setting of high pastures and seep willows, reeds, rushes and thistles that had already started to dry out. Everything burned like tinder.

In the corner of the valley Pablo could see a truly infernal scene where the wild mares had formed a semi-circle, kicking at the flames instead of taking flight. He watched as the thicket burned quickly and began to form a garland of fire so fierce that the most startled mares finally turned their backs, kicking out even more, while the voracious fire, advancing in front of them, reduced their manes and forelocks to ashes.

Then the flames from each end of the thicket mingled together and dark bodies in the centre were seized with panic, snorting, stumbling, falling over, getting back up only to fall down again in a fearsome turmoil. A plume of black smoke speckled with burning embers rose high above the mad frenzy, and countless red-hot splinters were scattered in all directions by the horses' furious hooves, becoming incrusted in their necks and rumps like flaming horse flies.

Moments later, the column of smoke became denser and more opaque, and a strong smell of charred flesh spread through the air. The heroic struggle between instinct and death had come to an end in that fateful place. With his head supported by both hands, pale-faced and dishevelled, the singing gaucho could not take his blood-shot eyes off the scene. It was only when the fire, driven by the north-east wind, came close to the outbuildings, that he jumped on his horse and, raising his riding crop, he set off like a demon, streaking along the edge of the forest towards the Witch's Ravine.

Chapter Fourteen

We mentioned that Don Manduca Pintos had arrived at the ranch the previous night and that, because of this, Montiel had gone in search of his daughter, resulting in the violent scene in the valley and on the hillside.

Whenever the rancher from Río Grande came to visit he spent two or three days in the company of his friend, not only because of their business arrangements over the land they had jointly owned for several years, but also in order to strengthen Manduca's romantic ties with Soledad, who had been promised to him as a bride by her father.

Don Manduca was not a man who could charm with his conversation or his manners, but on the other hand he affected a certain sincerity which made him tolerable and almost acceptable to the girl. A number of gifts of dubious taste complemented his relative obsequiousness. Conversely, he was accustomed to display his amorous intentions on the basis that she would in time belong to him, and as a result Soledad would keep him at arm's length, in spite of which she made light of his indiscretions, doubtless because it had not quite sunk in what all that business of taking a man as a life-long companion actually meant.

Pintos slept in the same room as Don Brígido, so that their combined snores overcame any obstacle and found their way into Soledad's room, although she was well accustomed to hearing that symphony of grunts and groans.

On the night in question, the concert had been building up since half past nine. Soledad, still overcome by the impressions of the previous night's events on the hill was possibly the only one who was not asleep. What had happened had hurt her and left her feeling a little acrimonious. She felt a strange emotion that was neither shame, nor sadness, nor passion, but all three combined.

Her father had hit Pablo in her presence and had even called him a thief. Just the memory of that barbaric scene made her confused and angry. Then he had abused her verbally and would have punished her with his riding crop if Don Manduca had not held her in his arms and shielded her with his body. That had been terrifying and it had made her withdrawn. Her resentment endured. She was deeply mortified by the memory and she wanted to erase it from her mind. She could not, and this increased her sympathy and affection for Pablo; she would have liked to have been close to him, in order to console him. She began to think badly of her father and to hate Pintos.

The poor singing gaucho, so slim and handsome, so meticulous in his caresses that he exuded the passion and taste of wild honey from the mountain. And afterwards, he was as sad as a lonely little bird! Soledad could still feel his ardent kisses on her mouth, and she parted ever so slightly her bright red lips to savour their lingering aftertaste on her own. She felt her breast flutter as if she could hear, very close by, a love song whispered in her ear. And his manner of embracing her, making her melt and laughing like an innocent adolescent until she had felt powerless to resist him!

She could also feel the passion of his lips on her shoulder, and around her waist she felt the pressure of his slim, nervous fingers, holding her tight, like a guitar. And as she wrestled with these memories, she turned her head to one side with a sigh, and finally drifted off to sleep with an expression of voluptuous pleasure on her face.

It was nearly midnight when Soledad woke up with a start. Through the cracks in the window-frame she could hear the muted sound of numerous voices shouting. What could it be? She wiped her eyes, put on some light clothing, slipped her feet into her shoes and ran to the window, opening it with a tug.

She was suddenly hit with reality, suffocating with heat and smoke. She ran from her room and headed towards the outbuilding where the ranch hands slept, arriving almost immediately at the door and trampling over everything in the shadows. It was not her father's name or Pintos' that she called, but cupping both her hands to her mouth she summoned all her strength and shouted, grief-stricken, 'Pablo! Pablo!'

Her voice didn't reach farther than the numerous

sparks that flew out from the flames, only to suddenly fizzle out halfway through their flight path. All around her, the roar of people shouting grew louder. Then she searched through all the outbuildings like a mad-woman. Everywhere there was more and more fire and smoke, shouting, distant cries, frenzied snorting and loud explosions, as if out there in the valleys, the foothills and the mountains, man and beast were locked in mortal combat in the midst of the enormous fire.

Chapter Fifteen

Before Soledad had woken up and fled the ranch buildings, her father, a regular early-riser, had dreamed of a strange smell and an unusual noise in his ear. He sat upright in bed and concentrated. The noise coming from outside was not the sierra collapsing, but it was something just as formidable.

Without waking up Pintos, Montiel leaped out of bed to investigate the tremendous racket, and went out of the ranch house shouting orders, with a knife in his right hand. None of the ranch hands replied. Rather than wait for his ranting, some of them had preferred to escape, and others more faithful and spirited had decided to fight the fire, without waiting for his orders. Montiel was faced with a wall of fire. He shouted and screamed furiously.

There was an area of close-cropped pasture that surrounded the corrals, which had still not been affected by the fire. His horse was tied up there to a sturdy post. Montiel headed over to the post. He stammered out bloody threats and curses, sounding like a screeching cat. A multitude of small animals that had fled the scrubland close to the sierra crowded into the available space, scattering as he passed or running between his legs with a celerity born of panic, including guinea pigs, iguanas and silver-coated foxes.

The rancher dished out blows with a whip in his left hand and in his right hand a knife, rushing to get to his horse which was spinning in dizzy circles around the post, without managing to break loose from the training rope nor from the muzzle restraining it tightly at the other end.

The beast was snorting restlessly, adding to its twisting and turning while the training rope wrapped itself around the post, reducing his radius of action. When he reached five or six paces from the horse, Don Brígido returned his knife to its sheaf and bent down to take hold of the rope. His left sleeve was rolled up nearly to his shoulder and with his other hand almost twitching he searched along the ground for the rope.

He saw something black and twisting, moving rapidly near the post and thinking it was the training rope he grabbed it in the middle, taking care not to get caught and pulled over by an unexpected tug. But, at that very moment, what he thought was part of the training rope slipped through his fingers, writhing vigorously. It was a live body, thick and scaly, and its touch left him frozen with fear.

Montiel heard a high-pitched hissing and he immediately felt the reptile wrap itself around his arm and sink its fangs into him. What he had thought was a rope was a powerful rattle-snake. Enraged by the fire, the snake had accumulated a vast dose of fatal poison in its glands. Montiel gave a cry of anger mixed with pain and, using all the strength in his left arm he struck the reptile with a blow from his horse-whip but the snake, instead of abandoning its prey, slid lithely up his arm and bit him on the neck. It let out another hiss, wrapped itself round its victim's neck, and started to squeeze using its terrifying loops. Montiel, choked to death, opened his arms and fell to the ground. His bruised face looked horrific in the light of the fire and rivers of dark blood ran from his arm and neck. His eyes, bulging from their sockets, gave him the appearance of a strangled wild beast. His horse, which had managed to destroy the training rope with a massive tug, grunted and stepped over its master with a stamp of its hooves.

Chapter Sixteen

Although he had been fast asleep, Don Manduca Pintos heard Montiel shouting. The extreme heat had bathed him in sweat and the thick smoke penetrating through the cracks in the door and window frame made it impossible to stay in the ranch house. The man from Río Grande turned in surprise and called out in vain for his companion. He leapt out of bed and, only half-dressed, he went outside to search for his piebald horse. It took him some time to saddle up by the thicket. The smoke enveloped everything in a thick blanket, casting dark shadows, and the noise was tremendous.

Don Manduca finished his task without losing his cool and returned to the outbuildings searching for Montiel. He could not find him, and headed towards the valley, calling out his name like a barking dog. But his yelling found no response. A lake of fire stretched out in front of him, advancing ahead of the wind in a giant wave. The smoke pervaded the air, making it impossible to breathe and a million sparks flew up in a whirlwind, forming roaring vortexes, and between blood-red glows fantastic horsemen crossed back and forth like arrows, as if their horses had wings and snorted fire from their noses like apocalyptic dragons.

Pinto's loud shouting was met with other strange and

formidable sounds. Nobody heard. Isolated in separate pockets of land, enraged young bulls struggled in an instinctive response to danger. Mixed with the confused shouting of men there was a permanent braying, the jangle of metal, the crackling sound of the undergrowth burning and sugar cane exploding like bombs. Don Manduca retreated ahead of a stampede of furious young bulls.

Large clumps of burning ashes now began to fall near the fence, exploding like flying rockets. Pintos dug in his spurs, speeding towards the outbuildings. His horse flew along as if scared to place his hooves on the ground that was covered in flames.

'Brígido!' he called out energetically and he repeated it three times at the top of his voice, calling in all directions. There was no reply, only the barking of the enraged mastiffs came from the other side of the buildings, almost drowned out by a hundred other noises as if from the depths of a cave.

Lost in the dense clouds of smoke, the rider was about to crash into the walls of the outbuildings, but the weak light of a lantern shining from inside the building allowed him to rein back his mount in the nick of time.

Suddenly, moving rapidly without wasting a second, the rancher seemed to have resolved to carry out a daring mission, given the vast scale of the disaster. Because, turning almost about face towards the ranch buildings, his piebald mount leaping like a mountain goat, chafing at the bit, he pulled on the reins with both hands in front of a door, positioned the horse abruptly with a brutal tug, stretched out his sturdy arm and seized a woman by the waist, her silhouette barely visible in the smoke that enveloped the buildings. His muscular arm lifted Soledad like a blade of straw and placed her on his horse's withers in the blink of an eye.

'Who is that manhandling me?' she asked, almost suffocating. The only answer was the bellow of an ox. After one last exertion, her head turned to one side in a faint.

The horse turned round with its double load and they commenced their escape towards the hillside. On one side the scrubland was burning and throwing off sparks like an enormous wick and its bright glow lit up the path by the prickly pears, along the hill's lower slopes. How could it have caught fire so quickly? Don Manduca was unaware of the answer. Within the area that was still not dominated by the fire the only thing that was burning was the corn silo that he had built, which was flaming like an enormous funeral pyre for the ranch house and its outbuildings, now converted into a tomb, or like a red altar lamp that had been lit to show the path of the fire amidst the shadows. In less than no time Pintos arrived at the bottom of the hill, filling his lungs with the less contaminated air.

But another terrible surprise stopped his horse in its tracks: the Witch's Ravine, rich in undergrowth, was burning across its entire length, consuming the vegetation like grains of salt and releasing from its depths fetid clouds that penetrated the atmosphere everywhere.

Faced with that impassable barrier and the deep ravine from which a thousand flames were already licking at the pastures in the valley, threatening to spread the damage to the higher reaches, to the area where they grew agave, and to the growing numbers facing the flames as they advanced across the vast plain. With the imminent danger of roasting to death, encircled by the horrific bonfires, exactly like religious pictures depicting hell, Pintos hesitated. Finally committing himself to an act of heroism he tried to find his bearings, looking for an exit from the tightening circle.

The heat was becoming unbearable and the sweat poured from Pinto's face on to Soledad's body. She looked as if she were dead. The opaque smoke swirled about, hugging the ground, and the horse, foaming at the mouth, whinnied in terror at the danger all around them, his mouth bloody and his nostrils wide open like the rings on a gas stove.

In desperation Don Manduca considered that their best option was to stay low, following the bottom of the hill until they reached the ford. Once across, they would be certain to be safe, because further on lay the sierra with its fresh rivers and uncontaminated air.

When he was ready to proceed, closing his eyes to the danger, he had to once again restrain his horse from bolting in response to a strange, muffled noise. Moments later a huge group of cattle passed by a few paces away from them in a frenetic stampede, making the ground shake, and the beasts, half-scorched, with their horns lowered, bellowed furiously at the edge of the ravine and finally hurled themselves into that purgatory in a huge mass, some surviving and others tumbling into the basin until their heaped-up bodies formed a few dark gaps in the front line of the fire.

They had instinctively made for the path that led to the opposite bank, that they themselves had forged with their hooves when they were on their way to the watering hole. Their bodies shuddered for a few brief moments in that part of the ravine and then dispersed the voracious flames as they writhed in agony, soon to lie still on their bed of burnt ashes.

The dizzying horde seemed to Pintos like a herd of monsters being tortured with whips of red-hot iron and foolishly, almost accidentally, he plunged forward towards the lugubrious bridge, the insatiable flames licking at the cattle's hides on all sides. Just as he was about to reach the improvised bridge he was struck by the idea of throwing off his pillion in order to make the crossing easier, but when he tried to do so a pair of arms – those of Soledad, who had regained consciousness as a result of the scorching atmosphere – held on to his waist like clamps.

Don Manduca dug his spurs into the side of his horse, which stumbled down to the ravine and twice tripped over the fallen cattle. Without letting go of the reins, Manduca persisted in his attempts to release himself from the girl's iron grip.

When Soledad felt a violent shove she let out a scream, a scream so heartrending that the horse made a determined push and in a desperate effort tried to reach the opposite bank, but its forelegs collapsed once more under the weight of its load. Don Manduca, seized by panic and giving full rein to his instincts grabbed Soledad by her plaits, shaking her with an irresistible force and managing to release himself from her arms, and pushed her off to one side. The young girl's body lay motionless on top of the fallen cattle, one step away from the flames. Her loud scream had been echoed by another, which sounded more like the roar of a jaguar than a human voice. In his delirium, Pintos imagined that it was the witch's voice, and as he peered forward through the smoke that had been cleared by the wind, he could make out a pale face with curly hair and a diabolical expression.

Chapter Seventeen

As Pablo Luna left his vantage point and went charging back towards the ravine, his head was in a spin. What was happening inside his head was similar to the scenes that had taken place in the meadow at Montiel's ranch. Along with his implacable instincts for killing and vengeance, the type that in an uncultivated individual never seem to be sated even in the moment, transcending those of a brutish wild animal, his impetuous mind was also struck with a vague sense of nobility, fleeting recollections of his fervent passion that, prior to consummation had been so pure and simple.

Dark thoughts filled his mind, while others gave it light, like stars shining through the cracks in a stormy sky. One moment he was howling with laughter and the next his eyes filled with tears; he roared with anger, then softly whispered a name; his cruel laugh became a sudden lament; unbridled fury turned into the most profound tenderness. Through a series of intense emotions, the only thing he was aware of was the hatred that he felt in his heart towards others, and the deep love that he felt only for one woman who was alive and another who was dead. Soledad and the Witch shared the healthy side of his suspicious heart: an inexpressible longing and a sad memory; a passionate young woman and a frozen mummy.

Persecuted, hemmed in and brutalised, arson and murder meant little to him. No one had taught him any other rules and nor did he suspect that any existed. Nor did he believe that love could be half-hearted. Both hatred and love should be as vast as the desert. The morning light that was now racing across the valley could not penetrate a wilderness as enormous as the nomadic gaucho's yearning to be loved.

When he felt this desire, he could jump over blood and flames, but he was also beset with the call of vengeance. This call resonated brutally and relentlessly inside his head. At the same time, another voice told him quietly that his future would be one of sad loneliness, for all his life, if he did not drag another soul along with his, even if that meant being lost, like a pair of disoriented glow-worms deep in the forest.

He laughed and cried as he rode wildly, with the burning flames on one side and on the other the lugubrious hillside. His mind wandered between the glowing evidence of his crime and the cold, mysterious darkness, calling back memories of Soledad and the Witch, uniting the living and the dead, harnessing his instincts in order to increase his energy and strength, as the contravailing forces came together and moulded.

Then came the doubts, his childhood fears in the midst of enormous deeds, the sins of his birth in the presence of the final drama. Dark clouds gathered in Pablo's soul and he tried to fight them off, contemplating the all-consuming fire with gritted teeth and stiffened spurs. His horse flew along the path wild-eyed, with its nose in the air. And when its hooves passed almost touching the flames, lighting up horse and rider in full detail, the fiery centaur roared all the louder. It became a race at breakneck speed.

They crossed fields in the midst of a thousand deafening echoes, bathed in red like mythical devils, coming up from the ravine that had been transformed into a torrent of fire. They climbed the hillside, charged along the path lined with prickly pears and, surrounded by smoke and ashes, stopped in front of the granary. He set light to it. Clasping his horse's neck, he scrutinised the shadows, focussing on the movements at the ranch. He noticed Pintos riding with Soledad as his pillion and, certain that they would have to flee along the side of the ravine or along the side of the mountain until they reached the ford, because the cornfield, with its sheet of flames, cut off the exit on the other side or would force them to make an enormous detour, Luna turned round and, riding at full gallop, he crossed the valley and then the ravine at a particular place where it was still possible.

It was dark and lonely on the other side of the ravine, part foothill and part mountain. The singing gaucho dismounted and gave his horse a stroke. Then, without wasting another second, they rode down the path, already made narrow by the fire. Smoke was coming towards that area but at that particular moment the air was crystal clear, and one could see things normally at a reasonable distance. Pablo noticed Pintos approaching and he awaited his arrival with his *boleadoras* in his hand, expecting a confrontation.

Luna stood to one side as a group of bulls leaped in desperation across the ravine. He let the stampede go past and then scrambled back to the path which was now rammed with the bodies of the bulls that had fallen and, hearing Soledad's distressed voice, he replied with an intense, angry roar, jumping up and down with the agility of a jaguar. He was opposite the place where he had fought hand to hand with the wild dogs on the fateful night that they had caught the scent of the witch's scraps of food.

Seeing Pintos doubling his horse's speed over the dead bulls and the rider pushing away Soledad's body with an iron fist and a brutal shove, the singing gaucho dropped his lasso, unsheathed the dagger which shone with a bloody gleam, leaped down into the ravine and, seizing the terrified Pintos by his beard, he sank his dagger into his thick neck.

Showered with a warm flow that spurted from his victim's neck as from a strong, foaming spring, Pablo placed the knife in his mouth and with both hands he grabbed the rancher and threw him down into the flames of the burning undergrowth.

Pintos' bloated body fell head first into the fire's ashes

and was almost completely buried, the flames separating momentarily as if pumped up with a bellows, quickly closing again around him, growing in strength, the flames binding together, receiving the new source of fuel with a salvo of lugubrious crackles.

Pablo Luna lifted up Soledad in both arms with an indescribable speed, climbed up the steep slope on his hands and knees like a powerful wild beast dragging its prey to its den, finally gaining solid ground, standing tall, free, proud and victorious, expelling the breath he had been holding in together with his anger, his hatred and his love with a hoarse, guttural, savage howl. His sorrel horse snorted in shock.

A moment later, Luna made him feel his spur, heading with his passenger towards a mountain pass, leaving behind him a red horizon and mountains of ashes. Ahead of him the desert opened up, dressed in mourning at this late hour, the hills looming over it like muted giants.

And when, now far from the thick smoke, they could look up at a clear sky, its pale stars shone over the rider who was carrying on his back his guitar – the beloved confidante of all his woes – and in his arms a beautiful woman, the ultimate dream of his life, austere and proud, gradually advancing deeper into the forest, on an everlasting night full of solitude and mystery.

Select Glossary

- *Boleadoras* (aka *bolas*): a type of lasso made from three strips of rawhide, with round weights attached to each end, so that it wraps around an animal's legs when thrown.
- *Capybara*: largest living rodent, native to Latin America, also called *carpincho* in the Southern Cone.
- *Chiripá*: traditional gaucho blanket worn in the form of loss-fitting trousers, later increasingly replaced by *bombachas*.
- *La esquila*: sheep-shearing season.
- *Gaucho*: originally meaning 'orphan', an itinerant ranch-hand in Uruguay and Argentina belonging to a caste with their own dress code, values and customs.
- *Mate*: a type of infusion similar to tea, imbibed from a small gourd through a meta straw; much favoured in Uruguay and Argentina.
- *Poncho*: blanket with a central slit so that it can fit over the head and can be worn comfortably over the shouders.
- *Vizcacha*: nocturnal rodent native to the Southern Cone of America.
- *La yerra*: cattle-branding season.

**TALES FROM THE SOUTHERN CONE
AVAILABLE FROM THE CLAPTON PRESS**

<u>Translated into English</u>:

The Yocci Well by Juana Manuela Gorriti

Our Native Land by Juana Manuela Gorriti

An Oasis in Life by Juana Manuela Gorriti

Brutal Tales by Ernesto Herrera

Mysteries of the River Plate by Juana Manso de Noronha

<u>In Spanish</u>:

La Tierra Natal por Juana Manuela Gorriti

Su Majestad el Hambre: Cuentos Brutales

Los Misterios del Plata por Juana Manso de Noronha

Oasis en la Vida por Juana Manuela Gorriti

Lucía Miranda por Rosa Guerra

<u>Memoirs in English</u>

Rough Notes, Taken During Some Rapid Journeys
Across the Pampas and Among the Andes
by Captain Francis Bond Head

What One Man Saw, Being the Personal Impressions
of a War Correspondent in Cuba
by Harrie Irving Hancock

MEMORIES OF SPAIN SERIES
AVAILABLE FROM THE CLAPTON PRESS

Perfidious Albion: Britain and the Spanish War – Paul Preston

Forged in Spain – Richard Baxell

The Bones in the Forest – Michael Eaude

Never More Alive: Inside the Spanish Republic – Kate Mangan

The Good Comrade: Memoirs of an International Brigader
– Jan Kurzke

In Place of Splendour – Constancia de la Mora

Firing a Shot for Freedom – Frida Stewart & Angela Jackson

The Fighter Fell in Love – James R Jump

The Last Mile to Huesca – Judith Keene and Agnes Hodgson

Struggle for the Spanish Soul – Arturo & Ilsa Barea

Hotel in Spain – Nancy Johnstone

Hotel in Flight – Nancy Johnstone

Behind the Spanish Barricades – John Langdon Davies

Single to Spain & Escape from Disaster – Keith Scott Watson

Spanish Portrait – Elizabeth Lake

British Women in the Spanish Civil War – Angela Jackson

Boadilla – Esmond Romilly

My House in Málaga – Sir Peter Chalmers Mitchell

The Tilting Planet – David Marshall

Hampshire Heroes– Alan Lloyd

Remembering Spain: Essays, Memoirs and Poems on the
International Brigades and the Spanish Civil War – edited
by Joshua Newmark/IBMT

E5

The Clapton Press